A Farmer's Life
The Rivers Region Story

DAVID FAVOUR

ISBN:9798357331236

• <u>Dedication</u>

I dedicated this book to those who love peace,harmony,oneness and those who are into politics.

Table of Contents

Chapter 1

At six o'clock on a hot mid February Tuesday morning Thomas John Cowley is listening to the radio weather report while eating breakfast with his wife, Bernadette, and his thirteen year old son, James Thomas. Like all of the rural workers in the area they're paying close attention to the weather due to worries about the heat and possible fires. The weather people are issuing thunderstorm alerts for the region and the big worry is of a lightning strike starting a fire in the dry crop fields.

The winter started with above average rainfall, but it ended up with only half of the average. Spring started with double the average rainfall for September, but finished with half of the season's average. The initial rain caused a wild growth spurt, but the months of dry weather means it's all now a huge fire hazard. Due to political issues very little burning off was done. The environmentalists convinced the state parliament to pass laws limiting the burning off of natural growth, so there's lots of fuel lying around just waiting for a fire to burn. Adding to that are the crop fields. About half of the crops have been harvested but the stalks are still in the fields waiting to be dealt with after all of the grain is harvested. Any fires will be very hard to deal with, but the predicted thunderstorms and winds could have a fire racing across the fields like a rocket.

Like all rural areas there are no dedicated professional fire-fighters, just the Volunteer Rural Fire Service (RFS) made up of local farmers and staff. A call means they have to get in from their fieldwork to the fire equipment shed then out to the fire: the average response time is fifteen minutes in past fires and exercises. That's too long in most big fires.

Getting up from the table Tom gives his son and wife a hug and kiss each before driving over to see what his boss wants done today.

Arriving at the main equipment shed of the property over the road, about three minutes' drive from the farmhouse Tom rents, he parks and gets out. He finds his boss where he expects to find him, in the shed doing a final check of the equipment for use today before taking it out. Tom calls out, "Morning, Bob, what's on the agenda for today?"

The farm owner, Bob Watt, calls back, "I'm taking the header down to the back field. The used Army fire-truck I bought arrived last night. I want you to get it out and check it over. Fill it with fuel and water then make yourself familiar with it. I've got a feeling we'll need it soon."

"Right. This the one you were talking about that's set up for remote operation of some of the deluge hoses?"

"Yep. Make sure it works and is ready to use." Tom nods. Like Bob, he's worried about high winds, dry grass, and fires. By the time Tom is in the cab of the fire-truck Bob is driving the header out of the shed.

Five minutes later Tom has the fire-truck beside the water tank while he fills the large on-board storage tanks as most of the vehicle is water storage tanks to supply the two deluge fire hoses mounted just behind the truck's cabin. The tanks take a lot of water, so he has plenty of time to check the tyres, oil, movement of the hoses, and operation of the auxiliary engines. He even turns on the pumps to check the hoses work. By the time the truck has a full load of water he's happy it's in full working order, and then it's over to the diesel tank to refuel.

After refuelling Tom checks the radio gear all works and it's set to the frequencies the locals use. All OK. That didn't take long and there's a lot of time to go before lunch. Now it's time to get familiar with it, so Tom drives off across the paddock to see how she handles the fields and the local roads. While he drives in the open field he practices with the remote controls that operate the electric motors to aim the hoses. Damn, it's hard to drive both the hoses and the truck. He soon learns to set the hoses and to then focus on driving the truck. It really needs two people to work it.

Just after nine o'clock the radio goes again, "General alert. Small fire caused by lightning on the east side of Bennett's Downs. We got it under control." By nine thirty another six small fires are reported as being started by lightning. Tom reviews the calls in his mind and he realises there's a trend there. The fires are moving across the district in a south to north line. Stopping the truck Tom gets out of the cabin to climb on top of it. In the distance, well to the south, is a long wide line of thunder-heads with a lot of lightning activity in them. He gets down and he goes back to refuel and refill with water because he doesn't like this at all.

By ten o'clock another twenty-six small fires are reported as being dealt with by farm resources. Then the trouble starts. At ten fifteen the alert is, "General call. Major fire at Isaac's Plains. RFS needed."

Tom is reaching for the radio when it comes alive again, "Tom, Bob. I'm near the RFS shed. I'll get this organised. You stay there. I don't like this. Way too many fires and that's at the far end of our area. I don't want to leave us too open."

Tom grabs the microphone, "Bob, Tom, roger that. Will hold." He's not happy about not attending the fire as he's the second in charge of the local Rural Fire Service Team, second to Bob. But he understands what Bob's worries are, so he'll stay to cover the needs here.

Five minutes later the radio announces the RFS is on its way. Ten minutes later the radio announces their arrival on site. After a few more minutes Bob is calling for more help from the next district south of them.

- Runaway

Tom is very worried. If Bob is calling for more help then the fire must be big. He waits, listens, and soon learns the fire front is over a kilometre wide when Bob calls in both the neighbouring RFS units at that end of their zone. He's also reconfirms for Tom to hold where he is.

While he sits in the idling truck Tom thinks about the situation, then he starts to swear when the truck rocks in the heavy wind that just reached him. He thinks, Damn, with this wind pushing it if they don't get the fire under control the whole district will be burnt out by dinner time.

Tom drives to the fuel depot to refuel the tanker. He doesn't need to yet, but he's making sure he's got full tanks just in case he needs it. When he gets back on the truck he looks over to the south east and he sees a huge wall of smoke with the red flickers of flame in it. It's too far for him to make out the red lights of the fire-fighter's vehicles while they fight it.

Climbing into the cabin his hearts stops when the radio goes off, "General emergency. Multiple fires at Masterson Downs. Need RFS."

Another voice comes over the radio, "Major emergency. Wildfire, wildfire at Masterson Downs. Half a click wide and racing. Evacuate all north of the station. Get out while you can. Repeat, get out now!"

Tom jumps out and gets on top of the truck's cabin. He looks to the south and can see a large wall of flame racing toward him. The nearest help is a good thirty minutes away. He looks at the farms and he can see people scrambling as they dive into vehicles to get out while they can.

Turning to his right Tom sees a sight to make his blood freeze. The kids and mothers at the local school are in the yard having lunch. It's obvious they've not heard the alert.

Jumping into the truck he puts it into gear and he races off to the small local primary school.

While racing to the school Tom flicks on the state wide fire service radio and announces, "All units, general emergency. Bennett's Road RFS has an uncontrollable wildfire and is declaring a general evacuation for all areas north of the Bennett's Road control area. Get them out of there."

While racing across the kilometre to the school he hears the radio confirmations from the other districts and central command. He hopes they can organise a response to stop this before the whole region goes up in flames. But now he's got a bigger worry: a school full of kids to save.

He thinks about the fire while driving, there's no way he can save the school, he'll be flat chat keeping this truck and the bus safe with this single unit. Then he realises there's one way, and only one way, he can get them out. The fire is already going so fast they won't be safe going north and no time to get clear to the east or west, so the only way out is to go south, through the fire wall and to get behind it as fast as they can.

Reactions
Everyone in the yard looks up when the olive Army fire-truck roars in the gate and comes to a tyre screeching halt on the edge of the yard. Tom turns on the truck's public address system, "Everyone, we've a major fire. Forget everything and get on the bus. I can only get the one vehicle out, so all of you cram aboard the bus."It's a good thing they all know Tom and know not to argue when it's about a fire. The kids drop their toys and food to race for the bus. A few mothers head toward their cars, so he adds, "I said forget the rest. Get on the bus, screw the cars. You won't have a chance in them." One very stubborn teacher hops into her sports car and she speeds down the drive. The others turnabout and race aboard the bus.

Within two minutes of arriving Tom is leading the bus down the drive while he talks to the driver on the radio. The bus hasn't had long enough for the diesel engine to warm up properly, so it's a bit sluggish, but it will be much better in a few minutes. Tom says, "Janice, the fire is big and flying along. We can't hope to outrun it to the north, east, or west. Our only hope is to go south to bust through the firewall. Stay on my tail. As we get closer to the fire get as close as you can. I'll set the hoses to spray water out in a fan to cool the air around us to keep us as safe as I can. The worst part will be the firewall, as that's the hottest part. The danger is I don't know how deep the area of fire behind the firewall is. This is our only chance, so stick close and pray. Shut all of your windows."

"OK, Tom, good luck, and let's go," is her reply.

They don't have long to worry because the road here runs north south and when they turn right onto the road from the school access driveway they're heading at the fire at almost the same speed it's heading to them. The very speed of their approach will help them pass the firewall, but the fire zone behind it is a big worry.

Tom activates the radio again, "Jacko, are you and your people still at Masterson Downs?"

"Yes, Tom. We're following behind it, putting out what we can."

"Go to Bennett's Road and see how far along it you can get putting the fire out. I've got a fire-truck and a bus load of kids, and our only hope is to bust through the fire to the south. If you can shorten the area on fire right beside the road you'll help us a lot."

"OK, we'll get over there. It should only take a couple of minutes to get there because we're in the big wheat paddock beside the road at the moment."

Two minutes after leaving the school Tom sets the hoses onto wide spray at an upward angle of forty-five degrees and he starts the pumps. The water goes out in an area twice as wide as the truck and about a third higher too. The spray is falling just in front of the truck and it's being blown back over the truck toward the bus, creating an oval shaped envelope of cooler air without flames. Just seconds before he enters the firewall Tom can feel the cooling effect as soon as the water starts to fall. Then the air gets a bit warmer. Both the truck and the bus are going as fast as they can. Janice keeps calling to tell Tom she can go faster, so he's been speeding up and they're now over eighty kilometres per hour when they enter the fire which is racing north at about the same speed.

In a flash they're through the front of the firewall, the hottest part of the fire and into the burning fire zone it's leaving behind it. The smoke and flames from both sides flow across the road and make it almost impossible to see. Their only real saving grace is the road here is dead straight for several kilometres and Tom hopes to be through the fire before the next set of bends because that can get real nasty real quick

The fire seems to be thinning out when Tom crashes into a burnt out wreck on the road. The sheer strength of the truck and its speed gives him a moment to deal with the situation when he turns to push the wreck off the road while speaking on the radio, "Janice, go round on my right. I've hit a wrecked vehicle, don't hit me." He listens to her acknowledge the order while he also listens to his truck protest the damage to it. It's not steering well and he can feel it dropping to the left while it slows down, despite him pushing down on the accelerator. So he thinks the tyre or wheel on that side is done in.

Making a snap decision Tom activates the radio, "Janice, floor it. I'll spray you from behind while I can." He reaches for the hose controls and sets them for a concentrated spray while he aims them to fall just in front of and on the bus.

Janice has a hard time getting the words, "Roger that," out past the choking in her throat as she understands what's happening in the truck.

A small hand takes the radio off her and James Cowley activates it as he starts to sing while crying. He, too, understands the meaning of his father's last transmission, "God be with you 'till we meet again,..."

All those on the frequency understand what's happening and they all keep quiet while the boy's clear soprano sings the hymn. After a few words Tom's baritone joins in with, "... 'till we meet, 'till we meet, 'till we meet at Jesus feet,..."

The bus moves forward with the spray of water moving over it in an erratic manner while Tom adjusts the angle, distance, and strength of spray along the road to stay with where he thinks the bus is. The falling water hits the bus often enough to keep it safe and cool enough for the passengers. Just as James finishes the first verse the bus bursts out of the fire zone and into the pocket of doused fire created by Jacko and his workers. Jacko waves them on down the road so they can concentrate on trying to get to the truck in time to save Tom.

Hearing this Tom puts the hoses back onto spray and aimed above the truck. This cools much of the area around the truck, but it's already sustained a lot of fire damage and the heat is very severe.

The bus pulls up down the road, well behind the fire, while James finishes the hymn. He releases the button on the radio. A moment's silence, and then they hear Tom, "The Lord is my shepherd, I..." and it goes on until " ... my cup runneth o'er..." as the radio goes silent when the truck's radio antennae melts from the radiated heat of the fire.

After a minute's silence James picks up the radio again and he starts to sing again, "Mine eyes have seen the glory of the coming of the..." When he finishes the final verse of the Battle Hymn of the Republic, his father's favourite hymn, he drops the microphone while his body heaves with his sobs. Janice turns in her seat and hugs him to her.

While Janice holds James she says a short prayer of thanks for Tom's help, and she hopes James' mother, Bernadette, is safe and sound in town or somewhere else.

About half an hour after the breakout Janice takes the bus and all of the passengers to her home as it's just down the road from Masterson Downs. They get out and go inside. Many of the women have cell phones so they call other family members to let them know they're safe and to learn how they are. The others use Janice's phone to call family. Janice is worried when she can't get a response from Bernadette's cell phone.

All of the children are tired from the events, James more than the rest and he's almost asleep on his feet. Janice makes him have a shower and get dressed in some clothes belonging to her son who's about the same size. Within half an hour of arriving at the farmhouse an exhausted James is asleep in her spare bedroom.

By mid-afternoon the local Country Women's Association has a call centre set up in one of the Bowen's Creek Council meeting rooms with a dozen phone lines manned by volunteers. Different whiteboards list missing people, known to be alive but away from home and the known dead. No answer from Bernadette's phone two hours after Janice gets home, so she has Bernadette Cowley listed as missing.

Nightfall sees all of the state and national emergency support services on site in the area because the Australian Army and Royal Australian Air Force provide transport to get them to the affected area. Tents and food arrive by the truck load to house and feed those without homes now.

The next morning Janice calls Bob Watt to see what she can find out about Tom's family so she can contact them. All of the employment information Bob has lists only James and Bernadette as next of kin and they can't think of any more. She wants to pass James on to his relatives since she has no room for him to stay with her for more than a few days.

It's near lunchtime when the local police tell Bob they've identified Bernadette's burnt out wreck of a car with what they think is her body. With this information Bob calls on Janice to collect James and he takes him home to his house. He's got plenty of room because the large house has been all but empty since his wife died a few years ago and many years ago his five children left home to start their own families.

The house James' parents rented from Bob is destroyed in the fire. However, Bob's house, two kilometres further east, is untouched by the fire due to a wind shift pushing it a little to the side before it reached there. This leaves James with only the clothes on his back and the change of clothes Janice gave him.

James has nowhere else to stay and no living relatives he knows of. He just stays on with Bob while things are sorted out by others. The situation is still unchanged several weeks later. For some reason neither seems interested in making any changes to the situation.

Despite James being an orphan no one informs the Child Welfare people about his situation. James calls Bob 'Pop' because he's near the same age as many of Bob's grandchildren who live interstate. When they have to complete paperwork for the government Bob takes James into the city of Rivers to the Centrelink office and helps him with it. Due to how they interact the staff assume Bob is his maternal grandfather and they note the 'fact' James is with his grandfather on their file. This error helps with processing the paperwork and it also helps to keep the Child Welfare people out of their lives because the government computer records show James is living with a close family member. None of the bureaucrats think to do a detailed records check on the family or their relationship.

Note: The paperwork they lodge is to change the Commonwealth Government Student Support payment for James to go direct into his own bank account which he already has, and James also lodges claims for Commonwealth Government Special Support payments to those who lost their residence and clothes in the fire.

- Aftermath

The fire races across the state all afternoon and it takes another four days to be put out. Seventy-three people lose their lives in the fire, most in the first few hours while it moves faster than they can get out of its way. The Coroner's Enquiry determines the main cause of the fire getting out of control is the amount of natural growth fuel along the several watercourses on the property Masterson Downs. The owner is found to be blameless due to the laws in place as the evidence includes his fines for removing more of the natural growth than he was allowed by the current laws. Estimated property damage is over one hundred million dollars.

The political fallout of the event results in a change of government at the state election later that year, and a change of the laws involved.

The body of the teacher who ignored Tom is found in the burnt out wreck of her car only a few kilometres from the school.

Local fund raising activities are held to assist those who lost their houses or loved ones in the fire. Insurance companies are quick to pay out claims for death or property damage, due to government pressure.

The students of the Bennett's Road School attend the Bowen's Creek School for the rest of the year. The replacement primary school will take until Christmas to be built and made ready.

Although it costs more than buying another used one does, the locals clean up and rebuild the fire-truck Tom drove and name it Tom's Tanker. A new Rural Fire Service facility is built at Bennett's Road and it's named the Cowley Centre with a plaque about Tom mounted in the entrance way. The previous facility was burnt down in the fire.

The next year, on Australia Day, Bob takes James to Canberra so he can be presented with the Valour Cross the government awards Tom for his actions in saving the bus load of children that day. It's a very solemn trip for both of them, both going there and returning to the farm.

Chapter 2

- Adult Employment

James finishes high school in October, several weeks before he turns twenty. Despite having lived in the area since he was seven he has few friends, other than those who live on the neighbouring farms. So his twentieth birthday is a very small gathering at Watt's Here on the Sunday afternoon nearest his birthday.

While he thinks about what to do for a living James continues to work for Bob after finishing school. He can't afford to go to university due to the living costs and having no way to pay them, and there's no point in staying on at the farm. Two of Bob's grandchildren are interested in the farm as a way of life; their parents aren't, but they are. Over the years Bob's children and grandchildren often came to visit or stay at the farm for holidays. Bob enjoyed their visits and he now really enjoys teaching two of them how to be real farmers. but neither want to be first to say so. There's a strong bond between them from all their years together.

After a few months of talking to people and researching jobs James does a lot of thinking, then he decides to join the Army. It gives him a chance to do something for the country while learning more about the world and picking up some other skills. In October he visits the Army base near Rivers and he learns how to join. One oddity is he has to drive to Canberra to sign up and then he'll be sent papers to attend the base at Rivers for basic training, because that's where they do it.

• Army Life

James meets the rigours of Army recruit training without complaint because he sees it as an essential part of the job. While other recruits are busy complaining he's busy studying what he has to learn to be a good soldier. His quiet assurance and willingness to just get on with what he has to do is noticed by those supervising the training and put in his file.

Like all things the training comes to an end and the recruits are sent to various units where they get more training relevant to their duties there. For some reason unknown to James his platoon Sergeant takes a personal liking to him and that, along with his good performance as a soldier, is enough to see James promoted to corporal when they have an open position for one within the platoon.

Just over two years into James' service his unit is sent to Afghanistan. Soon after arriving there Sergeant Parson has James go with him on a visit to another base in the city they're in. James is sent in to get the Supply Officer to come out to talk to the Sergeant waiting in the vehicle. James is a bit worried about this, until he sees who is being led to the counter to see him by the private James spoke to at the counter. The Warrant Officer stops and asks, "You want to see me, Corporal?"

James smiles as he says, "No, Sir." The WO is turning to look at the stunned private when James adds, "My Sergeant does, Sir. He told me to come in here and, I quote 'get that lazy supply officer to come out and speak to me here,' end quote. He's outside while keeping an eye on our truck." The WO is getting real angry about this until Jim adds, "However, Sir, I think your brother is trying to set us both up."

The Warrant Officer stops, looks at him and says, "My brother!"

"Yes, Sir, Sergeant David Parson. I don't know why your names are different, but you look so much like him the relationship is clear."

Warrant Office Richard Bourne laughs, "Dave isn't my brother, we're close first cousins. Our mothers are twins." With a large smile he adds, "Let's go see him," and he walks around the end of the counter.

The two cousins meet and Richard tells Dave about the way James greeted him. They spend the next half an hour in the nearby Sergeants' Mess catching up on news etc. After that Warrant Officer Bourne takes Parson and James over to a nearby US Army base to see a friend of his in their supply unit. James and Sergeant Parson leave the building with a new US Army issue 9 mm automatic, webbing with shoulder holster, two spare magazines, and a few boxes of ammunition each.

For the next six months James' unit provides escorts for convoys on supply routes around the countryside without any troubles. The small convoys have two squads as guards while bigger ones have the whole platoon or a couple of platoons to guard them, it varies with the size and contents. But, like all things going well, when trouble starts it's big.

Corporal Cowley is in charge of a squad of soldiers in the last truck in the convoy while Sergeant Parson commands the detachment from the lead vehicle with another other squad in it. Like all of their runs where the Sergeant is the one in charge he spends time checking the vehicles while unobtrusively securing a package of explosive to its underside and he hands James a radio transmitter to detonate it. Parson calls it a parting gift, if they get taken out in an attack to get the supplies this gift will see they don't get the trucks or most of the supplies. The trip today is a regular run to villages along a safe route, so no trouble is expected by anyone. Like their company commander often says, "We're going with the convoys because the orders have all of the convoys go with guards."

The convoy leaves before dawn and, an hour after their lunch break, it's almost to its first destination when the lead supply truck suddenly stops. Naturally the rest of the convoy stops behind it and the Sergeant has his vehicle turn around to come back. The driver of the stopped vehicle is out and has the bonnet up like there's an issue with the motor.

There's something about the way the driver keeps looking around the area that worries James so he exits his truck while saying, "Right, everyone out and set up about the vehicle. I don't like this." In seconds his men are out and spread out on the road around their transport. He's on the radio informing the Sergeant about his actions and concerns when four rocket propelled grenades fly out of the rocks to the right of the road to slam into the guarding troop carriers, two per truck.

Because Sergeant Parson also has his men out and deployed most of the troops are out of the vehicles when the rockets hit, but the drivers are still in them. Three men are killed and two are wounded in the attack.

Parson is walking back toward the stopped truck to see what's up with it when the rockets are fired. The blast behind him causes him to stagger forward. The driver of the stopped vehicle turns to run into the field beside the convoy, heading toward where the rockets came from. Parsons brings his rifle up, aims, and fires at the driver. The running man screams when the rounds rip through his lower body while tearing apart his groin and inner thighs. Parson smiles at hitting where he aimed while thinking, No paradise for that treacherous bastard!

The Australian soldiers take up the best defensive positions they can on the ground around their Land Rover troop carriers while they search for targets in the surrounding fields, firing when they find something to shoot at. Two men in the field stand up in a depression to fire two more rockets and are knocked backwards by the soldiers who see their upper bodies and shoot them. One rocket is fired downward at an angle to hit the ground several metres in front of him while the other fires when that man is falling onto his back. This rocket goes straight up until the propellant runs out, then it falls back down a little behind where the man fired from. The rocket explodes when it hits the ground and a few screams are heard from that part of the field to make the soldiers smile.

The situation soon becomes worse when a large number of armed men move across the field from boulder to boulder while shooting at the soldiers as other men shoot from cover to protect the ones moving. The return fire from the soldiers ensures many of the moving men don't advance any further, due to the soldiers' bullets renovating their chests.

While this is happening the other local drivers are quick to get down from their trucks and run away across the field on the other side of the convoy while they head away from the attackers. The men aren't armed and the two damaged Land Rover Perentie series troop carriers stop them from going forwards or backwards so they're getting away from this as quick as they can, because this is their best option in the situation.

James is careful while moving around to check his men. He moves a couple of them back into the damaged Land Rover because it gives them better cover than lying on the road and it expands their field of fire due to being about a metre higher than lying on the road.

The Land Rover transports are disabled and damaged, so are their long range radios, but the extra ammunition and supplies in them are still OK. Thus they can sustain a long combat, if they have to. One task James does is to pass ammunition from the truck to the men.

All of the Australian troops are worried because this is a small convoy on a route where there's been no trouble before and they're now under attack from a very large Taliban force. They know it's a large force due to the number of enemy they've already killed and the number who're still shooting at them from the field. Both NCOs are worried because the enemy has taken some heavy losses, but they're continuing the fight.

Several minutes into the fight James is on the left side of the Land Rover loading up a bag with loaded magazines to hand out when shooting starts behind him and he's hit in the left thigh. Turning while he falls he sees a group of half a dozen men attacking from the previously safe side. He hits the road and he switches from the three shot burst mode to full auto. Holding his rifle level with the road he swings it along the line of attackers, and he smiles because their height differences sees the men being raked across their thighs and groins with his long burst. They all scream while they drop to the

 A moment later there's no sound of movement around James so he raises his upper body to look down the line of trucks. All he can see is truck wheels in a sea of feet for as much of the convoy he can see. He has a huge grin when he points the detonator toward the supply trucks and he pushes the button. Five loud explosions rip through the air at the same time as the blast shock wave bounces off the road under the trucks.

The Taliban officer leading the attack is very angry with the heavy losses inflicted on them by such a small group of soldiers and how long it took his men to kill them all. Walking in behind his men he wonders how many bullets they fired because the ground is littered with the expended cases. Reaching the men at the back of the convoy he orders them to get in and on the supply trucks so they can drive them away to their new base they're establishing near here. He takes a moment to walk the length of the five trucks while he checks the supplies in them.

Reaching the front truck the officer orders some men to move the bodies out of the way while he opens the door to climb into the truck and leave. He has one foot up to step into the truck when he's tossed forward and to the side by an explosion. Lying on his back he looks back along the convoy to see all five of the supply trucks are wrecks and what's left of the supplies is spread out over a large area. Much of the food in the trucks is now destroyed by the explosions while the rest is thrown out and around. He goes to get up, but he can't get his right foot under him. He looks down to see why, then he screams when he finds his right leg ends just below the knee and blood is pouring out. While he reaches for a field dressing he faints from the blood loss. Like a lot of his men who survived the battle and are wounded in the explosions the officer dies before anyone who's able to help him can give him first aid.

Of the one hundred and fifty Taliban members who start the attack on the convoy about fifty of the attackers are killed in the attack with about forty wounded. Many are killed in the bomb explosions while many more are injured and bleed to death before the fit survivors can help them. The defenders and bombs leave only thirty-eight live attackers.

Ten minutes after the explosions the officer who started the day as seventh in command learns he's now the one in charge and he's the only properly appointed officer left. He orders the men to check everyone, to collect all of the working weapons, ammunition, and as much of the food they can carry. It takes a while for so few left to check so many dead.

Eighty-five minutes after the attack started the surviving victors walk away from the scene while heavily loaded with only a very small fraction of what they went there to collect by force of arms. They aren't happy about leaving so many of their dead comrades behind them.

Aftermath

James can hear the enemy talking while they move about, from the tones of what they say he's sure they aren't happy with the trucks going bang in their faces. He's happy because he can see so many of the enemy lying around and not moving. After some time he hears the voices moving away. Lifting up a little he peeks over the edge of his hole. He can see a group of people with heavy loads about a hundred metres into the field, and all are walking away from him. He lies back to rest while they get well away. Being very tired he soon falls asleep.

The sounds of people talking and walking around wakes James, so he rises up to look around him. He sees a group of women and children walking about the road and fields while they collect what they can of the supplies the convoy was carrying. Lying back down he goes back to sleep because he doesn't know if he can trust them or not and he isn't ready to take the risk.

Base
Late in the afternoon the radio operator at base realises he hasn't had a report from the convoy, so he transmits a request for them to call in. Several minutes later the communications duty officer lists the convoy as out of contact and he sends in a request for an aerial check of their line of travel while he also lets Command know of the situation.

At five p.m. an Unmanned Aerial Vehicle (UAV: a radio controlled plane with a camera, also called a drone) is circling over the scene of the battle after flying over their travel route from the base. The televised images are being seen by a number of officers while they discuss the situation they're viewing.

Arrangements are made for a replacement convoy to leave the base in the morning. It'll have an extra company strength force go with it to investigate and clean up the combat site. The investigating officers going to the scene are briefed and they're given all of the details of the convoy guards and drivers before they're finished for the day.

Next Day
The next morning the double convoy departs on time. When they reach the combat area the supply convoy leaves the road to detour around the area by passing on the left of the road, about a hundred metres into the field, but only after it's checked for explosive devices and other types of booby-traps.

The troops of the investigating force dismount to spread out to check the area while they set up a secure perimeter around the combat zone. With them properly deployed the two investigation specialists dismount to walk over the scene, taking photos and notes while they try to work out what happened at the site.

Being under the damaged troop carrier gives James some protection from the elements, but it was still very cold during the night. Also, in the heat of the battle he failed to properly clean out his wound before he put on the field dressing and the wound became infected by the germs in the dirt he fell on. Now, almost twenty-four hours later, he's running a high fever and he's not fully aware of his surroundings.

Thirty minutes into their investigation the officer signals for the troops to collect the dead soldiers and to move the dead enemy to the side so they can clear the road. A platoon doesn't take long to place all of the convoy dead in body bags and lay them in the back of the truck brought along for this task. When they bag the dead the names of the soldiers are given to one of the investigators.

Captain Harrison checks his list of those in the convoy against the list of the dead. After double checking the lists he orders a private to count the bodies. Everything checks, except they're short one. He turns to the other investigator to say, "George, ignoring the local drivers we expect to have ran away, we've accounted for all of our people except Corporal James Cowley. The soldiers and the distribution team are all here, except Cowley. Should we be concerned about him?"

Captain George Kable, Australian Army, turns to his US counterpart and replies, "I checked all of their files last night. None of our people are a risk, so we should only be concerned about what they're doing to him, if they got him alive and took him with them." He glances around the scene and adds, "It looks like they really paid the ferryman. But I do wonder about who blew up the trucks and why they did it. I can't see the Taliban putting in this much effort unless they were after the trucks and supplies."

"Yeah! I guess we'll never know about the destruction of the trucks."

Kable turns and signals to the troops cleaning up to get to work on clearing the road by loading the damaged vehicles onto flat-bed trucks. A wire cable is attached to the damaged Land Rover and a recovery truck winches it back down the road to load it for taking back to base. If it can't be properly repaired it can be stripped for parts. When the truck is about three metres back
down the road from its original position the hole James is in is now visible and one of the soldiers helping to guide the truck while being reeled in spots the hole and its contents.

The private calls out, "Hold it, we've got another one," and everyone turns to stare at him while he walks over to where the Land Rover was and he looks down at what he's sure is another body. The feverish James isn't aware of his surroundings but the removal of his shade lets the hot sun beat down on his hands. His helmet is covering his face but the heat on his hands makes them uncomfortable and he twitches. The private sees the small movement of the fingers so he races closer while shouting, "Medic, he's still alive!" Two medics and both investigating officers race to the spot to see what they have.

While the medics move James out of the hole Captain Kable is busy taking photos. Captain Harrison looks at the private who found James and orders, "Place someone on each corner of where that truck was." He raises his camera as he gets ready to take photos while the private puts three others

Kable waves a private over to collect James' gear while he takes a moment to gather his thought. "Sergeant Cowley, I don't know how long you'll be before the doctors clear you as rehabilitated and not in need of hospital or rehabilitative care, but the doctors here tell me once they get you well enough to discharge you from the hospital you'll also be discharged from the service on medical grounds." James' head whips around and up to stare at Kable. "The muscle damage from both the bullets," on seeing James' eyes flare he adds, "Didn't you know you got hit with two bullets in the left thigh?" A head shake is the reply. "Well, two bullet holes, damage to both major sets of thigh muscles, and the further system damage from the infection means you've lost too much of the power and control of the left leg. No matter how much you recover you'll always have a limp from now on so you're fitness is down and you won't be passed as combat ready."

James is very thoughtful while he this all in as he slowly nods in response and he thinks, Now what do I do for a living? Oh well, first is to get as fit as I can!

The plane back to Australia is loaded with troops going home, all of them with someone waiting for them, except Sergeant James Cowley.

For twelve months James is in hospitals and medical facilities in Sydney undergoing rehabilitative training to build up his muscles. Then back to his home unit in time to pack up all of his personal effects and to be discharged fourteen months after being shot.

James isn't happy at being discharged from the Army after only a few years of service. He knows the Army pension will be enough to live on, but he does want to do something with his life and he now has to re-evaluate what to do for a living

Chapter 3

James settles in well, almost like a member of the family due to the time he spends at the homestead: all of the meals plus many evenings for James and Al to discuss the farm. The two houses are only twenty metres apart, so it's no issue. There's even a protected walkway between the two that crosses the back of the double garages attached to the side of each of the houses.

The work on the farm goes ahead steadily. The orchard is cleaned up and expanded, so is the range of fruit planted in it. None of what is in the fields at the moment is worth trying to harvest or use as anything except fertiliser, so they cut it down and plough it into the ground. This is done as part of breaking the soil up for planting crops again. The land is almost as hard as rock due to the long time without planting. At this point the only land they don't plough and break up is at the houses and work buildings, even the orchard gets a light workout with the plough in the areas between the trees and tree rows.

The soil reports are back and examined: all of the fields are good to grow any crop they want as an organic crop. Deciding what to plant and how to set it out takes a lot of talking while they do other tasks. One task they do while talking about crops is to remove all of the old fencing. Only a few of the steel posts are any good for further use. All of the wire is rusty and beyond help while the wood posts are old and rotted, so it all comes out. Whatever can be reused or recycled is set aside while the rest is properly disposed of.

The plans for the fields are to set out two sets of seven fields the same size for the crops, another for the houses and work buildings, one for the orchard, and the end field that's for stock grazing because it'll be too much work to clean up and set up for planting and harvesting. This is due to the creek and rough areas in it making it hard to work properly.

During this time the council negotiates buying a strip along the front of Right Here for the road expansion. It's easier to buy Al's land because it's less work to shift the fence line due to it being replaced. The council surveyor is quick to peg out the new front fence boundary so James and Al can put the new front fence in to mark the new roadside boundary. The fence and gate for the stock field is next up, going along the top of the creek's gully on the crop field side, thus giving the stock access to the creek for the length of the stock paddock. They put in the orchard and house fences, then those for the fourteen crop fields: seven fields of equal sizes on each side of the access drive. To simplify access each is a long field running back from the drive with gates opening to the drive from each field, there are no gates between the fields. The fields will be worked in a seven year crop rotation the way it was done for centuries, until a few decades ago.

Most of the local farmers grow either wheat or canola; a rapeseed plant grown for cooking oil. Due to the local large amounts of both grains Al decides to avoid them and James agrees with him. They'll be growing legumes and hay grasses for part of the cycle, but the main crops they decide to grow are sunflowers for their seeds and corn.

Al and James get on with preparing the fields, building the fences, and getting the orchards ready. Much of the time it's James showing Al how to do what needs to be done, but neither man has an issue with the way things go. The work proceeds at a good pace while they get the farm up to scratch as a commercially viable operation.

Firearms licences are issued for both men and they have to buy a gun-safe to keep them in before they get approval to buy a couple of shotguns and rifles for use in reducing the wild animal pests. Over the time they spend getting the property ready they supplement the larder with rabbits and roos, which then requires James to teach Jean, Jenny, and May a number of ways to cook the animals for meals. He concentrates on stew variants first, because they're a lot easier to cook right.

Family Affairs
About six months after James starts work Jean's younger brother, Dave, turns up wanting to stay there on holiday. After a week Dave asks about staying there full-time as he had a falling out with his parents.

Al asks about making Dave a hired hand. James says, "Let him live with you and let him do household chores. But, for heaven's sake, don't hire him or pay him a wage. Not if you want to keep the farm."

While giving James a frown and a hard look Al asks, "What do you mean by that?"

James sighs then says, "Dave is as lazy as hell. That can be dealt with. He's also terminally stupid, that can't be worked around. In a science fiction book I read as a kid they had a quote: 'Against stupidity, even the Gods strive in vain.' It means stupidity is not correctable. If you hire Dave he works for you and you have to worry about worker's compo for him. When, note: when not if, he fucks up you get to pay for fixing it all and looking after the bugger for life or he sues your arse off. Family living here do not get worker's compo, but a hired hand does. Protect yourself and your family, don't hire him. Let him stay and be a bludger while you try to get him to find work in town or on another farm."

That night Jean and Al have a long talk about Dave. Al is surprised to find Jean agrees with James about not hiring Dave. So he ends up staying with them while supposedly looking for work with someone else. Dave pays some money as board to cover food and utilities costs, then this is all put down in the farm books as a revenue source along with some estimated charges for his food and utilities costs. This is all checked and approved by Al's accountant in town.

Jean finds time to speak with Bob. She learns all about the death of James' parents and how he lived with Bob afterwards.

Life and work moves on with everyone except Dave working hard. Al and James work the farm while Jean, with the kids helping her, work the house and orchard as well as the kids doing their studies.

Girlfriend?

On a more personal note: despite the ten year age difference Jenny sets her sights on James as her future husband, and he's oblivious to her intentions. Watching her set about taking control of James' life gives Jean and Al a lot to talk and laugh about when by themselves. At first Al isn't so happy about the situation, but Jean talks him around to accepting it. The fun thing for them is how clueless James is about it all. Due to the way he lived with Bob, and followed by the Army, James never did get much of a lesson about male / female relationships, or how to develop and build them.

James usually spends Saturday afternoon at home because he isn't involved with any of the local amateur sports clubs and he doesn't go to any of the games of the town teams, either. He isn't sure about how it happens, but after a few months of living at Right Here he's spending most Saturday afternoons taking all of the Porter kids into the city of Rivers to watch an afternoon movie or to do some shopping. Jenny is the one to organise the trips and she's in full control of the people on them. The other kids are used to Jenny being their boss and they're very amused by the way James does as she says as well. While James simply goes with the flow of events because he sees no reason to do otherwise. Anyway, they all usually have a fun time in the city.

A few weeks after Dave starts living on the farm Jenny has James on a shopping expedition to Rivers that's just the two of them. It's only when they walk into a furniture shop he decides to act and he asks her, "Jenny, just what are we shopping for today?"

She smiles at him as she replies, "Decent furniture for the house you live in. It needs to be properly furnished."

One of the shop staff joins them as he asks, "Who's paying for this?"

"You are, because it'll be your furniture."

Giving his head a slow nod he says, "And if I don't want to pay for a lot of new furniture because I'm happy with what little I have?" The part statement and part question hangs in the air for a moment.

With a sigh Jenny turns to him, "Jim, you need the furniture so you can have guests around to visit. You don't even have a proper seat for you to sit and watch television, let alone something to sit on when you manage to have a girlfriend visit your home."

"I see no problem yet, because I don't have a girlfriend. But I don't suppose it'd be a problem to get some furniture now. That doesn't tell me why you're in charge of this expedition."

"That's real easy. I'm in charge because you've no idea of fashion or what suits a room's décor." The shop staff member is amused at how this conversation is going.

"OK! But no dining room table or chairs because I plan on making my own from the trees we cut down."

Jenny's eyes go a bit wide, "You know how to do that?" He nods yes. "OK! No dining room set, for now."

They spend the next couple of hours looking at furniture sets for the lounge room, bedroom, and a cheap kitchen table set. Jenny even picks bedding materials. She only grins when James sighs and says, "Anyone would think you're choosing all the furniture for your house, not mine." Which makes the shop assistant smile, because she realises that's what Jenny is doing and she can tell James doesn't realise it yet.

The trio are busy writing up the order when the store owner walks over to speak with them. He grins as he says, "Hi, Jim. Haven't seen you for a long time. I heard you're in the Army!"

James turns to face Mick Green. He takes the offered hand to shake it, "Yeah. I signed up for ten years, but I got medically discharged a little while back. Now I'm working for Al Porter on Right Here. What are you doing now?"

Mick smiles, "I own and run this store." He turns to the assistant, "Gayle, give Jim the full staff discount on what he buys." The assistant, Gayle Davis, is surprised as she knows Mick is very tight on discounts.

Ten minutes later Jenny and James are walking out the door while Gayle asks Mick, "How come the discount for Jim Cowley, Boss?"

"We went to high school together for a few years. The school had a bully who was a few years older than Jim. On both the first and second day of school the year Jim started he punched the hell out of the bully when he picked on Jim. The two incidents caused the bully to review and change his behaviour, and there was no more bullying after that. I figure a lot of people owe Jim for those incidents."

"What happened to the bully, Boss?"

Mick grins, turns to her, and says, "I now run a furniture store." Her eyes go wide while he walks back to the office to work on the accounts.

Because Jim said there was no urgency on the delivery they aren't delivered until several days later when they have another delivery near Right Here. The driver and his helper have no trouble unloading the gear and Jenny, already home from school for the day, has no trouble getting them to put it exactly where she wants it. Later, James is surprised to see the house all set up when he goes home to have a shower before dinner. While he gets dressed he looks at everything and he starts to have a few thoughts about what Jenny is up to, despite their age differences.

While having a cup of hot chocolate after the meal James says, "Jen, I see you've all of the new furniture set up! Happy with it?" She grins as she nods yes to him. "Why do I have the feeling you're moving in soon?"

This causes Dave and the other kids to turn toward James. Jenny replies, "That could be because I intend to once I get the place how I want it. Nice furniture, nice curtains, etcetera."

"I like you a lot, but just when were you going to tell me this?"

"I had planned to do it when I took you to the jeweller to buy me the rings for my eighteenth birthday." The kids and Dave are stunned, Jean and Al are trying hard to hide their grins as James gives a slow nod.

"I see! In that case you better spend all of your free time with your mother while you learn to cook. I can't cook worth a damn and if you move in with me you'll have to do all of the cooking for us both." He gets a few stunned looks from everyone at the table. "I figure neither you or your parents are worried about the age difference, otherwise one of you would have said or done something by now. One other point, you know what I'm like so don't expect to change me, because it won't work."

Jenny has a huge grin at James' acceptance of her plans for their future life together as a couple.

The next afternoon Jean is showing all of the girls how to cook. Once the roast is ready and in the oven she turns to Jenny and says, "Jenny, I hope you're paying attention and do learn how to cook well. Forget what Jim said last night, not only does he know how to cook, I'm told he's really a very good cook. He paid for his board with Bob Watt for eight years by cooking their breakfast and dinner every day. He used to do some of the family meals before his parents were killed in a bushfire. I'm also told his mother had a few ribbons for pies Jim cooked and she entered in the annual shows. Think back, it was Jim who taught me how to cook rabbit and roo." All the girls are surprised, until they remember watching Jim teach their mother about cooking rabbits.

Over the next few months Jenny spends a lot of her time making curtains and organising everything else she needs to have the house 'just right' for them as a couple.

While she's busy doing that on the weekends and in her spare time James uses his spare time to ready some of the wood from the cut down trees from the orchard. The bigger tree trunks only provide two to four boards each, but all of the trunks are big enough for making chair parts. It takes a few months for James to cut the wood to build a nice table and eight chairs to go with it. He even has upholstered seats and backs for the chairs, a skill he learned when working on his car. The whole Porter family is very surprised by the results when he shows them.

Almost six months after Dave moved into the farm homestead Jenny moves out to live with James in the other house.

•   Fixed for Good

Several months after Dave moves in to live at Right Here James and Al are in the equipment shed carrying out routine maintenance on both of the tractors when Dave comes in to walk off with the gas welder and cutting kit. Both of them see him leaving the shed with the kit and Al calls out to him, "Dave, what do you need the oxy kit for?"

Dave stops to reply by yelling back, "Got to fix a bracket on my ute." Al nods yes and Dave keeps going while dragging the kit behind him.

Several minutes later both men stop what they're doing to go wash up for lunch. While walking out of the shed James turns his head to see what Dave is up to at his ute. The vehicle is about fifteen metres away on the other side of the dirt road through the farm. The ute is sitting on the cement slab poured for another workshop to be built on later. Dave is kneeling in the tray of the ute with the welding helmet on and working the torch on something near the front right of the ute tray. Both men take a few more steps before James' mind puts a few facts together and he spins round to take a closer look. Across the front of the tray of Dave's ute is a large silver Liquid Petroleum Gas (LPG) cylinder and Dave is using the welding torch on something right up against the cylinder. James yells out, as loud as he can, "Dave, turn that off and get the fuck away from there." All he gets for his trouble is Dave's left hand raised in the two finger salute. He never did like James telling him what to do.

James is about to race over and drag him away when there's a loud bang and a plume of white gas rises from the left side of the front of the ute's tray. James shoves Al toward the ground before he races for Jenny who's a few paces away and walking toward them. At almost the same time as Al hits the ground beside his old ute parked in front of the shed James hits Jenny with a full body check, wraps his left arm around her, and he tosses the both of them to the ground. In that same instant in time there's a huge boom from over near the ute Dave is working on. James is almost to the ground when something hits him hard on the back of the left shoulder and spins him a little. Thus, instead of landing on the right hand and arm he has braced for the impact he lands on his left shoulder. He hits the ground hard and it hurts him a lot.

James counts to ten slowly before he releases Jenny and says, "Jenny, go inside to check your mother and the kids are OK." She nods yes while she gets up on her feet.

Al is getting to his feet while looking at the mess that once was Dave's ute. On seeing the grass around it is on fire he races into the shed to grab one of the fire-fighting packs. He's soon busy putting out a bunch of small grass fires in the area around the ute.

When James tries to move his left arm or put any weight on it he has to stop due to the pain it causes him. He rolls onto his belly to use his right arm to get up. Once up on his knees he pulls out his cell phone, then he calls for an ambulance and the police. He takes his time getting up, so he reaches Al just as Al finishes putting out some small grass fires. Thankfully James and Al keep the grass down near the house, so there isn't much to burn.

James says, "Al, once you get the fires out get your camera and take photos of the scene from every angle. Also take shots of the shed, your car, and the house as seen from here. You'll need all of that as evidence. I called the police and ambulance so they'll be here soon. Get hold of your insurance people because they need to know about this."

Al glances over to where what's left of Dave is lying as he says, "I'll go stop the ambulance. There's nothing they can do for Dave."

"Fuck Dave! I want the ambulance for my shoulder, it hurts."

"What!" Al walks around James to look at his back because he can see no injury to his front. "Yeah! You'll need to go to hospital for that. The damn torch head is stuck in your shoulder. I bet that does hurt. What the hell happened over there?"

"That dumb bastard was using the oxy on something right up by the LPG tank. The heat would have caused the gas to expand. It eventually blew the valve off and let some of the gas out. I don't know if the rest of the tank failed or not, but when the free gas hit the flame of the torch it lit up and we got to experience an LPG bomb at a much closer range than we ever wanted to."

About fifteen minutes later the ambulance turns up, they check him, and James is taken off to the hospital for some emergency surgery plus a full check by the doctor. The police turn up at the same time and they ask what happened. Al tells them only what he knows about it in regards to Dave getting the oxy torch then seeing him in the back of the ute using it, followed by the explosion.

When they interview her Jenny says, "I was walking over to talk to Jim, almost to him, when he called out to Uncle Dave to stop what he's doing and to get away from the ute. Uncle Dave gave him two fingers. There was a bang and a white cloud appeared near the left of the ute tray, Uncle Dave was working on the other side of the tray. Jim pushed Dad down and raced to me. He grabbed me and threw us both to the ground. We were still in the air when I saw a huge flash of flame make a big fireball around the ute at the same time as there's a loud boom. I hit the ground. A moment later Jim let me go and sent me inside to check on the rest of the family. No one was hurt in there so I came outside again and Dad was busy putting out grass fires while Jim was talking on his phone and walking over to Dad with a thing stuck in his shoulder."

The police get James' statement after the doctors finish working on his shoulder. The doctors keep James in the hospital for two days.

A few hours after the event police specialists arrive from Rivers to check the scene. They take photos, interview everyone again, and take away the remains of the LPG tank from Dave's ute wreckage.

Damages
Dave's ute is a burnt out wreck, Al's ute has one side peppered with bits of metal, the equipment shed wall near the explosion has a lot of small holes in it and all of the windows on the side of the house nearest the bang need to be replaced: they got broken by the pressure wave of the explosion. James has a broken shoulder blade, a dislocated shoulder from the way he landed on it, and a lot of damage to the back of his left shoulder. James isn't happy when the doctor puts him on bed rest for a week with light duties for the next two months, which includes no driving of any vehicles for the two months.

Aftermath
While he's in hospital James has a long line of visitors to see him. All of the visits help keep him from being bored while there. When the doctors do get around to letting James out Al picks him up because Jean won't let Jenny skip school to collect James.

On the drive home Al briefs James on the outcomes to date by saying, "The police are still looking into things for the coroner. The insurance agent's been out. He refused to consider a claim on Dave's ute for the damage to it but he helped me write a claim against Dave's third party insurance for damage to my property and your injury. He's approved a claim for the damage to the shed, the house, my car, and the tractor." James turns and raises an eyebrow. "Yeah, we found the big tractor was damaged by some of the bits of metal, the little one was protected by the big one. He expects they'll write off my ute, and you're on compo."

James grins while he pulls out his cell phone. They both use the same insurance agent: Peter Marks. The phone rings and James says, "Hi, Peter, James Cowley here. Al Porter's ute. If they write it off find out how much I can buy the wreck for, please. I also want Dave's wreck."

Peter asks, "Why, Jim?"

"You know my big black beast, don't you?" When Peter says he does James adds, "It was a worse mess than Al's ute when I bought the wreck. I fixed it up and I can do the same to Al's wreck too."

Peter laughs, "Yeah! I'll get the wreck for you. With you doing the work yourself it becomes a viable repair, but not if you pay commercial rates to fix it. As to Dave's wreck. The company isn't touching it. No pay out means they don't get involved. Talk to his heirs."

"Thanks, Mate. I will." He turns to Al, "Dave's wreck is ours to do as we like with it. Much of it will be rubbish, but I think we can use a few bits from it, like the motor." Al nods his head in agreement.

"Jim, do you intend to fix mine and stick the motor from Dave's in it to make it more powerful?"

"I want to rebuild your ute as a car for Jenny. I figure to fix what I can of Dave's then see where we're at. The worst case scenario is we build it as a paddock basher. We can reach all of the farm paddocks without taking it on the road, so it doesn't have to be registered."

"Jim, right now I'm sure glad you talked me out of employing Dave. His parents are upset he's dead and Jean's angry they're upset. If he'd died while working for me I think they'd have sued me. As it is, they can't because all I did was let him borrow a few tools he said he knew how to use. They say they're deferring legal action until they hear what the coroner has to say. We still don't know what he was doing."

They talk about numerous other matters while they drive.

The workers' compensation insurance company pays James' wages for the three months the doctors have him off work before they pass him as fit to work again. This means Al has the money to hire some of the high school seniors to help around the farm. The pay-out for the repairs to the tractor, shed, and house is enough to pay for the parts and some people to work under James to replace the sheet metal plus do the lifting and holding while he does the fine work in replacing the broken windows on the house. The high school seniors are done for the year, except the graduation ceremony, so they hire some of the boys from the other farms in the area.

Note: Four months after the event the coroner holds an inquiry into Dave's death. After hearing all of the witness statements and the forensic report about part of the tank showing damage from the gas torch the coroner rules Dave died by Misadventure while making repairs on his own vehicle in an unsafe manner.

Dave's family aren't happy with his death, but they accept the report despite it making it clear Dave died because he did something he shouldn't have and he did it in a very stupid way.

- The Fruit Store

One morning Peter follows orders from the insurance company to drive out to make sure James isn't working on the farm while being paid compo. He laughs when he finds James sitting on the tail of his ute having a cold drink while giving directions to two late teen boys who are building a long shed on the edge of the farm land near the road.

When Peter explains the reason for his visit James says, "Well, as you can see, I'm not on the farm at all. Nor am I doing any farm work. I'm simply keeping an eye on these guys while they build a stall for us to sell the orchard produce from."

Looking at the sheet metal they're attaching to the frames on the ground Peter asks, "What's that sheet metal you're using?"

"We're recycling some we found in the rubbish pile, that's all."

With a big grin Peter asks, "Won't it leak with all those holes in it?"

"Nope! Once we have it in place we'll apply a weatherproof coating to the outside, we've already covered the inside of the holes with duct tape. Once it's up we'll line the inside with some good insulation."

While shaking his head at James building a market stall out of the old shed metal the insurance company ordered to be dumped Peter laughs and gets out his cell phone.

When they answer he says, "Lionel, Peter Marks here. I'm doing that follow up check you asked about. I drove out to the farm but Cowley isn't there. I found him down the road sitting in the back of a ute having a cold drink while watching some guys do some work on the roadside." He listens then adds, "The ute's parked on the road, not even on the farm. The only thing he's lifting is his right arm to drink from a cold can of Coke while he's talking to some friends working on the roadside. He hates sitting around and he doesn't like daytime TV, so he's out visiting and talking to keep from going crazy." A moment later he hangs up and he looks at James, "I hope you don't mind, Jim, but I just sent him some film footage of you sitting there watching the others working. That should keep them happy for a while."

James looks up, "Thanks, Peter."

"Oh, I almost forgot. They gave approval for you to have the wreck for two hundred bucks. I paid that from your trust, so it's yours. I hope that's OK. I couldn't find you when they asked for the money, sorry."

"I was going to pay from my bank account. But no worries."

Peter drives back to his office and James calls the boys over for a drink. All of the sheets are now attached to the five by three metre frames laid out on the ground around the five by twenty-four metre cement slab poured a few days ago. After a short break the boys attach strips to the edges of all of the frames. While they do that James is busy moving the one metre high barrels of coloured filler from the front of his truck's tray by tossing a web harness over them and walking backward while holding the harness ends in his right hand

It takes both of the boys to lower the barrels to the trolley they have for them, then wheel them over to the frames, one at a time. James stands and watches while he directs them in how to pour the contents into the frame unit without spilling it everywhere. This is followed by using a long-handled scraper with a metre wide blade to smooth the filler over the steel sheeting. Once the material is all spread out it doesn't quite fill up to the top of the strips attached to the sides. With that frame done they get another barrel to do the next one, until all of the eighteen frames are filled with the dark green tinted filler material. They're doing the work here because the finished units will be too heavy to move far after it's all done.

After their lunch break the teens get busy erecting the uprights by placing the prefabricated units on the bolts sticking out of the cement. The bottom plates with the bolts were placed in the right spots and the cement poured over them. The uprights are put in place and nuts to hold them down put on, but not fully tightened. The twenty-four metre long light-weight galvanised steel back beam is next. For the first time since this job started James has to get physically involved. The boys get the long beam up the ladders and set in place on the bolt plates. Now comes the reason for not fully securing the bottom nuts yet. James climbs a third ladder to check one end is on the bolts right before he loosely attaches the nuts there. He moves to the next upright, where he uses a rubber mallet to move the beam back a little until it settles on the bolts, then he attaches the nuts. On to the next upright he has to nudge the upright a little to get the beam to sit on the bolts and James puts the nuts on, then repeats on the rest. They do the same to fit the front beam. Now they put on the five metre long cross beams of the same material. James takes the nuts for this beam off bolts, the boys carry the beam up the ladders to set it on the bolts and James attaches the nuts. One at a time the nine beams are put on. Once everything is in place the boys go around tightening all of the nuts as tight as they'll go. James follows along behind to check they're tight. By dinnertime all of the frame is up and the panels are half cured, so tomorrow Al will use the big tractor to help them put the roof on and then put the wall frame panels into place

Chapter 4

Life Goes On

James is now over two years out of the Army and almost two years working at Right Here. He's not yet fully settled into civilian life, but he is settled into working on the farm. His life hasn't settled down yet, due to it being in a rising turmoil with the arrangements for his marriage to Jenny in the near future. Their farmhouse is set up how she wants it. He made the table and chairs, surprising many with the top quality of the work; although, considering what was done on the truck should have given them a clue. The farm is producing well as the first crops came in and sell well, so does the fruit from the orchard. The new trees are ready to have their produce added to the sales list and the large vegetable plot Jean started last year is now producing food for their store and table.

Despite the concerns and the early problems the farm is doing well. A lot better than Al thought it would, and most of that's due to James and his knowledge. The sale of the land for the road widening helped with cash for the infrastructure work which was more than Al had budgeted for, and the trickle of fruit sales has helped as well. But the big difference was the corn crop as the first one paid well and the next looks like doing better. It seems there's a higher demand for organically grown corn than there is for wheat or canola. The fields for the stock look good and they now have some stock in there fattening up for sale.

Right Here is getting a good reputation for tasty quality food that's going beyond their local area. The extra tourist traffic along the road helps with store sales too.

The store is set up beside the gateway into Right Here and there's no trees on either side of the road for a few hundred metres down from the store, just wild grass. So there's plenty of room for customers to park, but they have to be careful pulling over because of the roadside ditch before they can park on the light grass verge.

One Saturday afternoon James is watching the trouble some people have parking and he thinks about how to make it easier for them. While he's thinking Jenny makes a comment on the trucks just flying by and how it'd be nice to get their trade because there's so many of them. An idea springs to James' mind and he writes it down for later action.

The next week he goes to the shire council offices to speak to the shire planner, who takes him to talk to a few others. No promises are made, but they agree to look into his idea. Two weeks later a truck stops at Right Here and it starts to unload a large pile of concrete pipes just to the side of the gateway, but on the property.

Al is heading over to find out what it's about when James intercepts him to say, "Good! They're doing it. Al, this will be a bit of work but we want to do this, so let it be. OK?"

Al turns to him as he asks, "Do what?"

"A few weeks back I spoke to the shire council and offered to do the work for free if they'd provide the materials. The pipes are to go in the roadside ditches on each side of the road, then dirt over them and the ditches to build it up almost the same as the road but with a bit of a slope, and gravel over the lot. For a few hundred metres or so we'll have a car and truck parking area along the road here."

"Now why do we want that?"

"Easier parking and access for shoppers at the fruit store, meaning more trade and income."

"OK! I can handle the usual farm tasks for a few weeks while you get stuck into doing this. You asked for it so you do it all. Right!" James nods yes in acknowledgement of the order.

Over the next few weeks James is busy laying and setting drain pipe in the section of the ditches for one hundred metres on the Rivers side of their gateway and two hundred metres on the other. Every twenty metres also has a grill and drain at road level. When the grill areas are first put in he covers them with plywood then he puts markers on the fence to show where they are. Once all of the pipes are in a council officer looks them over before he organises the delivery of the earth coming from another road project. Putting it here means they don't have to pay to dump it. This is turning out to be a very cheap project for the council while making a major improvement to part of this road being upgraded.

While James is busy on the road Jean is busy making some changes to the store. She finishes before he does, so she takes time to add to their sign on the clear front wall. She now has healthy snacks plus hot and cold drinks available to customers, all from the farm produce. Even the bread for sandwiches is baked fresh that day by Jean.

James first does right beside the store, then right along one side of the road, getting the dirt in and packed properly before doing the other side of the road. The same with the gravel. For three hundred metres this section of road has an extra wide area to park on and an easier turning area for trucks to enter and leave the farm. Four weeks after he starts the work the parking and lay-by areas are finished.

James asks a couple of friends who are truck drivers to stop at the shop the next time they go by and to give an evaluation of the food and drinks. They do, and are soon raving about how tasty and cheap it is. After that there's a regular flow of truck drivers stopping for a snack and a drink. James has to make plenty of stools and a narrow counter he puts along the inside of the front wall so the drivers can sit down and eat in reasonable comfort while showing others the store is busy. The shop does very well with lots of revenue and a lot of profit, despite showing wages for Jean and the kids when they work in it.

For twenty-five metres each side of the gate James puts signs on the fence that read, 'Please park cars only in this area to allow good vision for the vehicles using the farm entrance.' The regular truck drivers who start stopping are good about parking a bit further away from the farm gate.

The Wedding
In late April Jenny and James have a small church service for family and friends. Well, that's how James asked for it to be. However, it turns out he has a lot more friends in the area than he realised. The invited guests number about forty, with a general invitation to all of the locals to be at the Saturday afternoon wedding and no one is to bring gifts.

The wedding date and time clashes with the opening game for the local football team which is not a competition game but just a warm-up game against another local team. So no one is upset when the start time is pushed back to an hour after the wedding, an event that surprises the Porters and James, but not Bob Watt or Peter Marks. They know how a lot of the long term residents regard James as one who's always willing to help, never complaining, and the son of the area's greatest hero.

The church isn't standing room only for the wedding, it's squashing room only with people jammed into seats and standing people pushed against the walls. The only place you can move is the narrow aisle left for the bride's entrance. The service is short, but the meet and greet afterwards takes a long time due to the large number of people there.

The only reason they can handle the crowd is because it's a nice day and they stay in the grass area beside the church while they meet and talk with everyone. The crowd thins a bit when the football teams leave to get ready, soon followed by their most ardent supporters. Three hours after the ceremony the crowd is down enough to let the couple depart on their short honeymoon. James will get the refreshments bill from the church ladies next week and he'll pay it then.

True to her word Jenny marries James on the first day possible after her eighteenth birthday, which was on Thursday. However, she has school on Monday and he has to work as well, so it's off to a hotel in Rivers tonight and back to their house tomorrow night.

Sunday morning the couple have a late brunch before checking out to go home. Each is handed a copy of the regional weekly newspaper and they're stunned by the front page picture of them leaving the church which takes up half of it. The attached text surprises Jenny a lot.

Local Celebrity Wedding of the Year

Saturday afternoon our local quiet unsung hero, James Cowley, a returned serviceman (medical discharge due to combat wounds received in Afghanistan) and farmer, married Jenny Porter, the daughter of his boss. Although several years younger than James our sources tell us she actively pursued him and had only a little trouble tying him down. He's quoted as saying, 'I'm marrying my best friend, what more can you want!' We agree with him. They made a lovely couple exiting the church (see photo above).

We found out they had thought to have a quiet ceremony with only the closest of family and friends, but word of the wedding got out to the general community. The church was jammed with well-wishers there to see them married. The only reason the local Fire Warden didn't do a head count and cite the church for too many people in the building was because by the time he arrived there wasn't enough room for him to be able to count those there. He had to settle for watching the service from the doorway.

The local football season's opening game between Bowen's Creek and Rivers North clubs adjusted the starting time of the game so the teams and spectators could attend the service. The organisers knew it would have been a double forfeit if they didn't let their people attend the wedding!

Young Jenny is a senior at Bowen's Creek High School and has been a resident in the area about two years, while James is ten years older and is a well-known local. He lived and grew up at Watt's Here from ten years of age until he left for the Army after high school, returning to the area when discharged. Shortly after his return to the area he started work at Right Here and has been a huge factor in its revitalisation and return to profitability as an organic farm producing a range of tasty foods.

Locals still remember the day James was orphaned by a bushfire and his father, Tom Cowley, earned the Valour Cross when he died saving a bus load of children while getting them safely out of the fire storm. We wish the couple all the best for their future.

Jenny simply stares at James after reading the article. He blushes and shrugs his shoulders, giving her a good idea why he's seen as a 'quiet unsung hero,' and she starts to eat her breakfast. On seeing Jenny start to eat James does too. Both are aware of a lot of the locals in the room looking over at them and smiling

The attention is too much for James, but there's not much he can do about it at the moment. So he simply tries to ignore it while getting on with his breakfast.

After eating they pack up, check out, and go home to start their new life together as a married couple in their home. Typical of farming life time off is very dependent on the needs of the farm, which has no real time off because something is always in need of being done on a working farm.

Making Changes?

Monday morning is a bit different with Jenny cooking breakfast for her and her man, she likes that thought - her man, in their own home. For the first time since she was given the car she drives herself to school, and causes a slight commotion when it's seen sitting in the school car park. The other girls are surprised she's at school, but they all accept the need for her to finish her studies. Changing her name and contact details at the office before class is a lot simpler than she expects as the clerk has the forms filled in and Jenny need only sign them. The rest of the school day is fairly normal with only a few comments on her wedding ring. This is because everyone she interacts with was at the wedding, as were most of the others from the school, and the rest saw the newspaper report of the wedding.

The day goes as usual for James with farm work until he's ready to go to town in the afternoon. Jean is going in to go shopping so she'll drop him off and Jenny will drive him home. They've an appointment with Peter and his wife: he's an accountant and she's a lawyer.

Jenny and James meet outside of Peter's office and go in for their set meeting with Peter and Amanda, Peter's lawyer wife. Most of what they want was conveyed to Peter and Amanda well before now. This meeting is to sort out the many legal forms and sign them now they're married.

A dozen documents are spread out for them to sign, wills for each, life insurance policies, and a power of attorney for Jenny to manage James' money. There's no problems with all the papers until they get to the last one, the power of attorney for the trust. Peter holds it up and asks, "Jim, before I hand you this form to sign I need to clarify a few things." James nods yes. "Those reports I send you on the trust, do you read them?"

"Sort of, Peter," is James reply. "Look, I'm good with my hands and what I know about farms, but those academic things are a headache. I got good marks at school, but I worked damn hard for them with a lot more studying than most of the other kids. I read what I understood of the reports then I put them aside. When I came back from the Army I had all those papers you gave me. I'm sure they're important, but all I could make out of them was you do better than average so I signed you up."

"I wondered if that was what happened. Especially when I spoke to you about the utes last year." He takes a deep breath, "The trust has a lot of money in it. Do you really wish to give Jenny full control of it?"

"Peter, I'm flat chat managing my pay each week. I can't handle the trust, so Jenny may as well look after it. I already have her managing all of the household bills. I suspect she'll let you do the financial wizard stuff on the investments and just keep an eye on it or get money when we need it. So I'll let her make that decision."

Handing Jenny a sheet Peter says, "Jenny, please look at this and explain it to Jim for me."

With a frown she takes the paper and looks at it. Her eyes go wide and she turns to James, "Jim dear, this report is the trust growth for the last six months. Have you seen one of these before?"

"Yeah. I get one every six months. I don't understand those long numbers so I look at the percentage. Because they're always in double digits and are growth, not loss, I just file it with the rest." Jenny and Peter just look at each other while Amanda wonders what it's about.

Jenny sits back to think on this, why can't he understand this. She asks, "Jim, what numbers do you fully understand?"

He grins, "Up to a hundred is easy, even a thousand is OK. After that, all I know is: it's a lot. As to money in the bank, I worry if it gets to less than four digits, after that I only worry if a shop rejects the card."

Peter shrugs, "Well, that explains a lot. However, I wonder how he got through the school system that way."

Amanda asks, "Why the big concern about this?"

Jenny looks up, "I'm ten years younger and I just found out my new husband has over a million dollars in a trust account as well as the sixty thousand he has in his bank account. I also found out he can't handle money above a few hundred. Why wouldn't Peter be concerned!"

"Oh!" is Amanda's only response.

James asks, "What's so important about a million dollars?"

Jenny grins, "With a million dollars you can buy a yard full of new cars, if you want to. Knowing you don't understand this explains why you work and why you're so careful with money."

"I work because I like working. When my parents died I had only the set of clothes I stood up in, and nothing else. So I soon learned to do without and how to make things go further. Now it's just how I do it."

"James, do you mind if I spend some money to help Dad with the farm?"

"Why not? If it makes the farm better it's better for us all."

Peter sighs as he passes the form over for James and Jenny to sign. When handing it back she says, "Peter, please keep managing the money the way you have been, but try and have a reserve available so if we need it we can get at it quickly. I think fifty thousand would be enough, if we need more than that I'm sure we can use the trust as security for a bank loan. I don't see us needing anything from the trust for many years, but I want a fall-back position just in case of an emergency."

While nodding his agreement he replies, "That's about how I've been doing it, in case James wanted anything. I couldn't understand why he never spent any, now I know. Now I'll send you all of the reports."

Next is the bank to have Jenny issued with a debit card and made a signatory on James' account as well as giving her Internet access to it. She opens a higher interest account and puts ten thousand across into it.

After the bank they go home. Tonight is dinner with the family. After dinner Jenny sits down with her parents where she has them explain the ins and outs of the farm operations and what they cost. When they go home for the night Jenny spends time on the Internet working out a few on-line courses to help her run the business side of the farm later on.

Doubling Up

The next afternoon Jenny talks to her father about the farm and how it's going. Al says, "Jenny, going on a strict operating cost basis I should be putting Jim on half days and half pay because we don't need to do so much infrastructure and repair work now. However, that'll cause him a lot of trouble. I saw how hard it was on him to not work when he was put on light duties by the doctor. So I'm looking for things we can do to help, even if they're long term items."

"Dad, the farm across the road is for sale very cheap. Why is that and is it worthwhile for us to expand by purchasing it?"

He laughs, "A good idea. I looked at it. The farm is very cheap as the last owner literally ran it into the ground. There's no equipment, the soil needs a lot of work, and so do the fences. It won't be able to provide an income for two or three years and it'll need a fortune of investment to do anything with it. That's why the bank has it at half the real value of the land. I spoke to them and they'd like me to buy it, but I haven't got the collateral for a loan to buy the land and to meet operating costs until it comes good. Getting that would keep us all busy."

"Have you spoken to Jim about Daisy Downs?"

Al smiles, "He raised the idea, but the bank shot it down."

"Call the bank and make an appointment for us to talk to them after school tomorrow. We want to talk to them about what you think you need, plus another ten percent for unexpected issues."

"Jenny, I've already done that and we don't have enough collateral. I've got a lot of equity in Right Here, but not enough to cover both of the properties. I'm about half a million bucks short and they won't take that sort of risk on Daisy Downs because of the past issues with it."

"Dad, trust me. Make the appointment."

Despite feeling it's a waste of time Al sighs as he nods his agreement to call the bank to go to talk to them tomorrow with Jenny.

The next afternoon Al meets Jenny at school and he takes her to the bank since she still catches the bus most days. They go in to see the manager about a loan big enough to buy Daisy Downs plus money for the farm operating costs of them both for three years. Placing a loan file on the table the manager, Mary Quinn, says, "Al, I know you can cover the repayments on the loan from your revenue but you can't provide enough collateral for such a large loan. Not on top of your current loan. Now, unless you've got something new to throw in we can't help you."

Jenny asks, "How about if Jim and I agree to guarantee the loan to Dad? Will that make a difference?"

"Jenny, it's nice for you to try and help your Dad, but he's over half a million bucks short on the collateral. Unless you have that amount of collateral there's nothing you can do. Head office wants more collateral."

While handing over the latest report from Peter she replies, "Why don't you look this over then ring Peter Marks to make arrangements for us to back Dad's loan. From what I've learned it's better for Dad to have one big loan from you than a couple of loans from different sources."

Mary glances at the report, at first, then she has a closer look before calling Peter to confirm the details. She discusses things with Peter on how to use the trust funds to secure the larger loan. Hanging up she says, "Right! Peter says you've the right to commit the trust and he has the authorities to sign papers. So we'll just get you, Al, to make the loan application. Jenny can sign on behalf of the trust as guarantor and I'll sort out the other papers with Peter. That'll take a few days to process, but since we're both the lender and the vendor it'll be quick so you can start doing what you want with it in a few days. I'll call when it's done."

Al is fast to fill in the paperwork and to sign where he has to, Jenny signs her part, and Mary signs hers. Al is still a bit stunned by this, and it's a little while before he asks, "Jenny, what did you do in the bank?"

"Dad, please don't tell anyone, but Jim has a lot of money in a trust fund. He works because he likes to, not because he has to. I've got control of the trust because that's what he wants. We're backing you."

"Why does he have you managing it?"

"Dad, do you remember that history show some months back where they spoke about ancient numbering systems and how early societies had systems that went from one to ten then many?" He nods yes. "Jim is a lot like that. He understands numbers up to about a hundred, but not much beyond that. He also has trouble reading and other things."
"But he's so good with the farm and equipment!"

"I don't understand it either. The long and the short of it is he's very good with his hands and the farm but a total loss on academic stuff. So I have to watch over the books and things like that for him. For all he's ten years older than me he's the innocent babe in the woods as far as life off of the farm is concerned today." Al simply nods his agreement again.

When they get home they tell James about buying the farm across the road. He sits down with Al and the map they have of it while they talk about how to repair the land and make it a going concern again. They soon have a set of detailed plans on how to work the land, lay it out for better usage, and rebuild the infrastructure of it. The one big help in all this is the land hasn't been used for four years, so it won't be that hard for them to get it organic certified once they get its soil fixed.

The work on Daisy Downs is very much a repeat of what they did to Right Here in the first year. The only difference being they know they have to add natural fertiliser and keep it fallow for two years before a cash crop can be considered. Within weeks all of the internal fences are out, the boundary fences are fixed, and the front gate is moved to now be opposite the gate for Right Here.

Chapter 5

A Time of War

Senior Constable George Rochester races out of the courthouse to his police car while talking on his radio. He soon confirms he's the closest to the farm with the fire. He's also a member of the local RFS so he has one of their radios as well. On the RFS radio he gives out the alert about the fire and its location while he starts his car, turns on the lights and siren, then he races out of town at high speed. Mark Meadows, the RFS sub-captain for that part of the Hartman RFS District lives on and works a farm near to the Johns farm, and he responds about heading that way.

Ten minutes later George and Mark are parked side by side on a hill and both are looking north toward the Johns farm. The town of Hartman is to their south-east and the fire is north-west of them, almost at the northern border of the Hartman RFS Control Area. Already the closest RFS units are at the fire. Unlike Bennett's Road all of the units here are located on different farms and the volunteers drive them to the scene. Due to the farms being so spread out this is a more efficient way to get them to the fires. The land here is wide open plains and the farms are a lot bigger than near Bowen's Creek.

Mark surveys the large triangle of burnt land behind the fire-front moving to the east. It's about half a kilometre wide and burned over a kilometre from the shed where it started. The hay-shed is still burning, but the crop fire is a much bigger concern as the shed has done its worst by setting the crops on fire and it can't do any further damage.

George asks, "Mark, is it my eyes, or are those trucks having trouble staying with the leading edge?"

Mark turns his binoculars on the RFS trucks at the northern and southern edges of the fire, and swears when he sees the men in them are bouncing around while spraying water from the tanks because the three trucks are racing to stay with the fire-front. He turns to his car, spreads the map on the bonnet, and pulls out his radio while looking at the map. After activating his radio on three frequencies Mark says, "General emergency, runaway wildfire Hartman RFS Control Area. Racing east with a wind from the west behind it. Evacuate all areas east of here."

George turns to his car to grab his police radio to spread the news and to get the police busy with evacuating people. While he does he hears Mark adding, "All town fire services stay in town and try to protect your towns by setting up protection on the west side. All Hartman RFS units north of town make for Little Creek Crossing to set up a safe zone on the edge of the village. Check farms and evacuate everyone to Little Creek as you go. It's going too fast for us to handle, let's protect our people, that's the best we can do with this one."

Right Here

James and Al are in the workshop completing the servicing of Tom's Tanker and its twin, Tom's Tanker Too, when the message about the fire at Hartman comes over the RFS radio. James pulls out the map and he sees Hartman is directly west of them, about twenty-five kilometres away. However, he knows how fast a wildfire can race, especially with the wind pushing it. Walking outside he feels the strong wind is from the west and that really worries him.

While racing for the detailed district maps James keeps in the RFS utility he has as the local RFS Captain he shouts out, "Jenny, Jean, take the two Tom's Tankers and fill them with water. Then race over to Daisy Too to soak all of the trees and the ground around them. Then get your arses back here after refilling the tanks. Al, race over to the RFS Shed and fill up every damn tank, sprayer, and bucket you can find." They all dash off while he spreads the map out.

After a moment he pulls the radio microphone out of the ute and says, "Hartman Control, Bennett's Road Command. I need the current location of the northern and southern edges of your fire and where it started from."

Mark responds with his best locations by estimating their distances from known crossroads then he asks, "What good is that?"

James responds, "I know the wind direction and this gives me an indication of where it's likely to hit us so we can concentrate on it there." Marking the three points James draws lines outward from the start point. Assuming it will spread at the same rate he extends the lines.

Mark comes back on the radio, "The wind and fire are picking up. It's moving east faster, but the sideways spread is a bit slower due to the faster forward speed." He gives the new north and south points, and they're within the lines James has on the map to make a narrow funnel.

Standing To

Lifting his radio James takes a breath then says, "Bennett's Road RFS Command is declaring a regional fire emergency and calling for all fire services east of Rivers Run Road and within half an hour's drive of the city of Rivers, town of Bowen's Creek, and the town of Carter to report to the RFS Command Centre at the entrance of the farm Right Here. If the wind doesn't have a major change of direction it will cross Rivers Run Road at Right Here in a path some kilometres wide. We need everyone here right now to prepare the roadside area to stop it. Bring everything and everyone you can." When he releases the button there's an orderly flood of responses from the local RFS and town fire services.

The local RFS and farm people are the first to arrive. James has his utility set up by the entrance and he's busy sending people to where they can be of use as soon as they arrive. Many have to park beside the road to wait for suitable equipment before they can get to work. Twenty minutes later people and fire-trucks are spread out over a fourteen kilometre section of the road, seven kilometres on either side of James' command centre. Jenny and Jean have returned and they're setting up the fruit shed to provide food, drinks, and a rest area for when it's needed.

The various tanker trucks are out dousing the roadside and as much of the crops on either side of the road as they can reach without entering the properties. James wants all of the vehicles to stay on the road to enhance the response times in moving about.

Mark Meadows is pacing the fire-front as best as he can and sending regular updates on the two end points. While the fire races closer to Rivers Run Road they tighten up the line because they can now narrow down where it will hit. The tankers and trucks from Rivers and the two towns are spread along the line because they've the biggest capacities and the strongest pumps. The six regional RFS units are all there too. So there's a very solid line of equipment and people along the roadside.

Disaster

James is starting to feel good about the situation as all of the people west of here have been evacuated east of their line, all of the road is doused, plus a few hundred metres each side of the road is soaked with water, and he has a solid line of trucks and people to fight the fire when it reaches them soon. Then his whole world is turned upside down. Police Officer Randy Davis looks up at James, "Just got word, five kids are still at the McClain Farm, a car is on the way to get them."

James spits out, "Shit!" while he spins for his ute. He jumps in and he takes off in a cloud of dust.

Al reaches for a radio but Jenny stops him, "Jim is driving the fastest vehicle in the area and he should get there sooner. However, there's no way he can sit here while some kids are in danger. Anyway, they'll probably need two people when they get on site." Al gives a slow nod in reply. He knows Jenny is right, but he doesn't like it and he can tell she doesn't like it either. However, both know Jim is his father's son, so there's nothing they can do about it.

After a couple of minutes' drive along Rivers Run Road James is in a slide while he skids around the turn into Bowen's Creek Road to head toward the fire. Just ahead of him is a police car with its lights and siren going. A little further down the road James blows past the police car like it's standing still. When the RFS assigned him this utility James had his mechanic upgrade the motor, now it's the fastest thing in the district. After two more kilometres James skids in the entrance to the McClain farm as he swears at the thick cloud of smoke and fire glare he can see over the ridge only a few kilometres further west. Flying down the long farm drive he hits the switch for his siren. A moment later he pulls up in a huge cloud of dust in the homestead yard to see four surprised kids standing on the back veranda staring at him.

Getting out of the utility he asks, "Is this everyone on the farm?"

The eldest, a girl, replies, "No, Annie is off reading somewhere. We've been looking for her to have lunch. She's not in the house or one of the buildings."

The police car pulls in behind James as he says, "Damn! OK! You four, in the police car and race for town. I'll look for Annie." James turns to the officer, "The bushfire will be here any moment, get these four out of here now. I'll look for the fifth." The cop nods yes while the kids race for the police car. In seconds the police car is on its way out at high speed while James is turning from his utility. He has one breather pack on his back, another on his left arm, and a pack with fire blankets on his left shoulder while walking toward the fields calling out, "Annie," as loud as he can.

For two minutes he's walking around the edge of the fields near the house calling out and not getting a response, then he hears a distinctive sound. A little to his left and ahead someone just popped open a can of drink. He races in that direction. A moment later he almost steps on a young girl about twelve years of age lying on the ground hidden by the crops and listening to music on ear buds while reading. The music is so loud he can hear it, despite the way she has them stuck in her ears.

Pulling the girl to her feet James hits the 'off' button for the music then he pulls the ear buds out. She starts to struggle, but stops on seeing his RFS jacket. Holding the breather set he says, "Quick, put your arms in this and strap it on." While she settles the breather set onto her back in a comfortable way he looks around and he isn't happy with what he sees of the situation due to the latest changes to the fire.

The fire-front is racing across the field toward them and an arm of the fire has already spread further ahead. His utility is on the other side of the several farm buildings to where they are and the fire is already between them and the truck with the workshop already on fire. There's no way out, so they have to find a place to hide from the fire.

Between them and the homestead is the sorting yards and beside the sorting yard is a loading ramp to help load stock onto trucks. The ramp is packed earth between brick walls. Taking Annie's arm James heads her to the east side of the ramp. On getting there he pulls out one of the fire blankets and he lays it on the ground with part of it up the wall of the ramp. He has her lay on the blanket in the corner then places two more blankets so their sides are between that blanket and the wall before he lies right beside her and pulls the three metre long blankets over them.

"Right, Annie. Put the mask on and turn the valve beside it on to the first click. That will give you a metered measure of oxygen despite no outside air. The blankets will protect us from the bulk of the heat, but it may still get very warm. We have to stay here until we're very sure the fire has passed over and is no longer active around us. The tanks will give us air for nearly two hours on the first setting." She slowly nods in reply. He sets his own mask in place then he reaches for the microphone of his belt radio. Holding it up near his mask he activates it and says, "Bennett's Road RFS Command, I've found the girl and we're caught in the fire, we're... , " and he gives a grunt just before he passes out.

While he's speaking to Annie the fire reaches them to set everything around them burning, except for the dirt ramp and their blankets. On the other side of the ramp is an old gum tree, very rotten and only just staying up. The fire weakens it further and the wind is enough to finally knock it over. The tree falls onto and across the ramp. One of the last remaining large branches sticks out enough to hit James on the head and knock his head into Annie's. To put his breather mask on James has to push his helmet back and doesn't put it on properly afterwards. The branch hits James on the back of the head, but instead of hitting the side of his helmet it hits the top of the helmet which has more protection. So instead of cracking his skull through the weaker side of the helmet the hit does no serious damage, but the force of it knocks him forward so his forehead hits Annie's forehead and both of them are knocked out.

Bennett's Road RFS Command

Al and Jenny smile when they hear James on the radio saying he found the girl, but are very worried when his transmission is cut off with a grunt of pain and is followed by silence. One of the volunteers calls out, "Here it comes." The yell moves along the long line of waiting people. They all take a deep breath, then they stand still while they watch an old and hated enemy come charging at them at full speed. It sounds like an old steam express train racing through the station when the fire-front races toward them.

It hits the damp crops in front of them and it staggers while it slows down. Al puts the RFS radio to his lips, "All tankers, hit it hard."

Twelve kilometres of road comes alive with the hoses on the tanker trucks working on the fire. Some are concentrated and aimed as far into the fields as they can go, spraying around as much as possible, while others are using a wider spray to cool the air and stop the fire-front.

For three minutes the two forces face each other, then the fuel at the fire-front starts to run out and the fire dies down a little. This is what the bulk of them are waiting for, Al gives the command and the ground troops slowly move forward to attack their old enemy. Backpack spray kits go into action when people set about putting out the fire at the ground level. The trucks move off the road and up to the fences to spray further into the fields. People move to gates and enter the fields before spreading out again, utilities pull up beside fences and people climb into the back of the utes so they can jump down into the fields.

Squad by squad, unit by unit, all of the ground troops advance and eliminate the enemy while some of the trucks move to the gates to move into the fields to advance on the enemy. The extra troops to the sides where the fire didn't reach are already moving in and flanking it.

Ten minutes after the fire reaches Rivers Run Road it's clear they're winning and soon mop up operations are all that's left.

Al is in command at the moment so he can't leave, but others do and Jenny is leading the race to the McClain Farm in her truck. She's followed by the two Tom's Tankers, a police car, and an ambulance. A few minutes later all five vehicles are stopped in the yard near the burnt out remains of Jim's RFS ute. Jack is standing on the roof of his truck using binoculars to scan the fields. He soon says, "Right, he has to be around the buildings. There's no lumps out in the fields big enough."

One crew sets to putting out the burning homestead while the rest spread out to look for James and Annie. After two minutes one of them spots the fire-blanket under the burnt out tree. After a few minutes of hard work the tree is out of the way, the blanket is opened, and they find the two unconscious people. Both are breathing and have pulses so they load them into the ambulance and both are off to the hospital.

Note: The RFS uses combined pumper / tankers for versatility.

Aftermath
Both James and Annie have concussions so they spend the next few days in hospital under close observation.

Many millions of dollars of damage was done to crops, sheds, and houses in the path of the fire. Due to the speed Mark Meadows declared the emergency people were able to evacuate in time. In a lot of cases the evacuation was only as far as the nearest village where they fought to keep the village fire free and all in it safe. James and Annie were the only people to be caught in the fire itself and they survived unburned.

The government holds a Royal Commission into the fire and the events leading up to it. Mark, James, Al, and all who held the line at Rivers Run Road are commended for their quick thinking and hard work. Criminal charges are laid against the four main players with Lewis, Johns, and Pike being sentenced to ten years in prison while Henderson is sentenced to seven years. The latter two appeal, but lose the appeals because they both knew they should have called in the fire while it was still small and could easily be put out.

Amanda Marks starts a class action against the insurance company for compensation on behalf of all who lost something in the fire. Her claim is based on the insurance company's stance to punish people instead of minimising damage. She claims Pike's action was a standard operating procedure within the culture of the company. The insurance company is quick to settle out of court and it's also very quick to pay up on claims by anyone who lost anything in the fire, other than the one by Johns.

The Daisy Too trees take only minor damage due to their pre-fire soaking. James' burnt out RFS ute is replaced and the wreck ends up in his workshop as another rebuild job, which Jim does very well on. Thus the Bennett's Road RFS ends up with another vehicle over their official list of equipment.

Note: A Royal Commission is an Australian Commonwealth or State Government investigation into a serious or major event.

Life Continues
Those affected by fire damage get busy in rebuilding or replacing a lot of buildings, equipment, and fences. The farmers work very hard at putting their properties back into proper working order.

What looked like being a thin year due to the extra-long dry spell and hotter weather than normal turns out to be financially better than expected. The average yield per hectare is down for all of the crops due to the weather problems at a critical time in the crop growth. This results in less produce for sale, plus the large losses due to the Hartman fire and other less dramatic small fires means the total crop yield is well down. This puts the per tonne price of what little is harvested higher than the previous year. Thus those who have valid insurance claims get paid out on the current price of the average crop yield. This helps cover a lot of the costs of the year's operations for many of the farmers affected.

Naturally the bulk of the money is invested in the preparation and planting of the next lot of crops. That's how farming is, this year's crop is harvested or finished so you start preparations to plant next year's crop.

Children grow up and people grow older while the crops are sown, grown, harvested, and sold. The many cycles of life go on.

Like Al and Jean, the cycle of life means James and Jenny watch their children go to school, then university, and some move away to work in other fields or areas while a couple of them stay to work the farms they live on. All are trained in the aspects of farming and farm life while they grow up, and they help on the farm until they move away.

Life is change and a part of the changes of life is death. Matt Porter dies of a cancer a few months before his parents' planned retirement. In an odd twist of fate when Al and Jean Porter retire it's Al and Jean Cowley who fill the gaps in the farm work. Al Cowley and his fiancé move into the house on Daisy Too because his studies concentrated on orchards. Al and Jean Porter move to the house on Daisy Downs while Jean Cowley and her intended move into the main house on Right Here because Jenny and James don't want to move house.

The new generation of farmers take over the main burdens of the farms while being directed and helped by the previous generation. This is the way of farm life where generation follows after generation. Time moves on and Al marries his Mary while Jean marries David to become Mrs Watt as David is Bob's great grandson.

The main driving force of the farms is still James with Jenny in full control of the books and the fruit shed. Al and Jean Porter still help out by working part days, or when there's a task where their knowledge or help is needed to do it right. The new couples have children and there are more than enough people to work the three farms well.

James is very annoyed by the changes in his physical capabilities as the years move on. Due to the damages done in his earlier endeavours he's no longer as physically capable as he was and the doctor is telling him to cut back on the physically demanding work of the farm. Despite knowing what the doctor says is true he wants to fight it, but he can't fight the doctor and Jenny as well.

On his fifty-fifth birthday Jenny sits James down and says, "Jim dear, you know you have to do less physically demanding work. The kids and grand-kids are more than capable of doing the farm work and now they only need a little direction from you. You've trained them too well. You now need to find a new challenge in life that isn't so physical."

He sighs then replies, "I know, Jen, I know. I don't like it and I've no idea about what to do now. I can't do anything that involves a lot of paperwork or reading, you know that. So what is there? If I spend all my time in my wood workshop we'll need to build a huge shed to store all I make. So what can I do?"

She grins as she hands him a USB drive while saying, "There's a few files on here I think you should look at. Then let me know how you feel about what they suggest."

He nods yes while accepting the drive. After the lunchtime birthday party James heads to his computer while the rest of the family heads back to the farm work. He spends the afternoon watching video files.

Changing Directions

Seven months after his birthday James is standing in the bedroom he added onto the house for Tom which is now converted into James' office. He stands in the middle of the room as he looks at the way Jenny has set it up for him. Slowly shaking his head he turns around and returns to the lounge room to look at the group sitting there. Jenny, Tom - who is home on leave from his work for four weeks, Al and Jean Porter, Al and Mary Cowley, Jean and David Watt are all sitting there, smiling.

After a deep breath and sigh James asks, "OK, my new office is set up for me to work in at home should I get the job. Now what?"

Jenny grins, "Jim, I'm more worried they'll give you the top job than if you'll get the job at all." He turns to her, "I've been talking to people about this for months. I've not done any real work before now because I wanted Tom back here to help direct us. Thus this four week blitz."

James turns to Tom and raises an eyebrow. Tom grins as he replies to the implied question, "Dad, getting you elected to the local council is going to be dead easy. Much easier than helping my regular boss get elected to the Senate, and he's well liked in the electorate. We've got four weeks to get your name and face before the voters who don't know you and to let the rest know you are really standing for election." James goes to speak, but is stopped by, "Dad, every farmer within ten kilometres of here will vote for you, so will all of the truckers who live around here, as will all of the RFS people. That's fifty percent of the voters right there, so it's clear to me you'll be elected."

James just gives a slow head shake as he says, "OK! You lot have it all planned, so just set to. Make no promises without clearing them with me first, and tell me where I have to be for what publicity events. Let's get this show on the road." They all smile and start taking turns to tell him what they've already arranged.

Publicity Launch

Late-morning of the next day, a Saturday, James is at a party for the members of the local RFS people and their families held in a major park in Rivers. The party is to start with a catered lunch he's paying for. The food is ready and the park is jammed with invited guests, including the local print and television reporters. Tom had much bigger plans for the day than James approved, when objecting to some aspects James said, "I know you've got to organise a few publicity things. However, they have to be done the way I'd do them, not the big and fancy stuff others will do. So no big stand, right!"

The result of that conversation is James climbing into the back of the burned out RFS ute he rebuilt. He has a microphone in his hand which uses radio to reach the several large speakers set about the park. Grinning, he turns it on and says, "OK, everyone. Please turn to face the pool complex." They turn toward him. "Good, now if you'll all keep quiet and pay attention for a few minutes we can get all the speechifying out of the way then we can get stuck into the food and drinks then the kids can play games. I'm sorry, but my campaign manager says I have to give a political speech so we can write all this off as part of my campaign, so listen up for a moment. I'm sure many of you know I'm running for the local shire council this year, if you didn't, you do now. I'm not going to make a lot of promises about doing this or that yet, mainly because I don't know what does and doesn't need to be done yet. Once elected I'll have the access to all of the information I need and I'll make decisions on the issues then. I do promise to do the best job I can and to do my best to see we get the best return for the money spent by the council. I won't be the only one on the shire council so I can't promise to do things, just to fight for them to the best of my ability. Please vote for me. Now, I believe that speech is long enough to qualify as a campaign speech, so you can now rush the food tables before the smell gets to be too much."

The crowd laughs while they move toward the long line of food tables to the side as James climbs down from the ute. In minutes there are orderly queues of people at the food tables and James is having a word with many people while he wanders through the large crowd of people present. At each table of food and drinks is a bucket with a sign saying, 'Donations for Jim Cowley's campaign, please don't put in any money unless you can truly afford to.' Some smile and drop a few coins in, some pass by without adding to the buckets, but that's as expected as James made a point of inviting a lot of people who are a bit short of money and he made a point of telling them not to donate.

The large crowd enjoys the food and the children enjoy the many games and activities set up in the park; including a range of jumping castles, face painting, various rides, even horse and donkey rides.

Jenny made a point of over-catering for the lunch, but she's surprised about how little food is left after the day is over and everyone is on their way home about four thirty in the afternoon. She turns to James, "Jim, they sure were a hungry lot!"

He laughs, "You didn't take a good look at them, did you!" She shakes her head no. "I figure we had about five hundred or so extras in for a feed. A lot of passing tourists pulled up and asked what was up. I told them to join in and enjoy themselves. Also, a lot of the Rivers locals called by to talk to me and I sent them over to get a bite too."

That night the news is full of James' campaign launch. The local television news is typical when the announcer reads:

Six months ago the nominations opened for the upcoming local government elections. Local farmer and RFS Commander James Cowley stood for the Bowen's Creek Shire Council. While all of the other candidates have been on the campaign trail for months the news from James has been quiet until lunchtime today when he had a campaign launch picnic in the park beside the Rivers pool complex. He gave one quick short speech and told everyone to have fun. Many people passing by were also invited to join in.

They show a video clip of his full speech.

After his short speech I spoke with Mister Cowley about why he left his campaign so late. He said, "Jenny is my campaign manager and she waited until our Tom was able to help her with professional advice. He's home for four weeks to help her out." Tom

Cowley is James' eldest child and also the campaign manager for Senator Murphy of the Rivers Region, one of our most vocal federal representatives. I don't know how well James will do in the election or how his short campaign will go with the voters, but those in the park today all said they'll vote for him. Like any campaign activity they had out buckets for campaign donation, but these ones had signs asking people not to donate unless they can really afford to do without the money. I even saw James stop a couple of people from putting money in while telling them to see to their family first. So it's clear he puts the people first.

THE End
Thanks for reading

BOOK BY THIS AUTHOR
The Wrong Way - or Is It? and Other

https://a.co/d/9Lulebhhttps://a.co/d/9Lulebh
Four stories with twists and turns - some adult concepts.

The Wrong Way - or Is It?
A schoolgirl wanders from her class in an ancient woodland and vanishes. The park has high security around it so it is impossible for people to enter or leave without it being recorded. Yet she has gone missing and is not in the park nor did she leave, what has happened to her?

The story was inspired by the cover image.

One Small Step
A student is to present his thesis and it raises a lot of interest before the results are made known. they all know he has a major revelation to present to the world.

The Truth About Paradise
Yes, the reports on the fate of the faithful in Paradise is true, but is it exactly what they expect?

Photographic Problems

A man helps a friend, only to see him tricked - twice. In each case he is able to turn the tables on the people causing the trouble. And in the process he and his friend find a very good life.

www.ingramcontent.com/pod-product-compliance
Lightning Source LLC
Chambersburg PA
CBHW080727120726
48001CB00010B/3166